If your child struggles with a word, you can encourage "sounding it out," but keep in mind that not all words can be sounded out. Your child might pick up clues about a word from the picture, other words in the sentence, or any rhyming patterns. If your child struggles with a word for more than five seconds, it is usually best to simply say the word.

Most of all, remember to praise your child's efforts and keep the reading fun. After you have finished the book, ask a few questions and discuss what you have read together. Rereading this book multiple times may also be helpful for your child.

Try to keep the tips above in mind as you read together, but don't worry about doing everything right. Simply sharing the enjoyment of reading together will increase your child's reading skills and help to start your child off on a lifetime of reading enjoyment!

The Mouse in My House

We Both Read® Book

Text Copyright © 2012 by Paul Orshoski
Illustrations Copyright © 2012 by Jeffery Ebbeler
All rights reserved

We Both Read® is a trademark of Treasure Bay, Inc.

Published by
Treasure Bay, Inc.
P.O. Box 119
Novato, CA 94948 USA

Printed in Singapore

Library of Congress Control Number: 2011935123

Hardcover ISBN: 978-1-60115-257-2
Paperback ISBN: 978-1-60115-258-9

We Both Read® Books
Patent No. 5,957,693

Visit us online at:
www.webothread.com

PR 11-11

The Mouse in My House

By Paul Orshoski

Illustrated by Jeffery Ebbeler

TREASURE BAY

Once there was a **tiny mouse**
that made its way inside my house.
And from its tiny little nest . . .

the **tiny mouse** was one big pest.

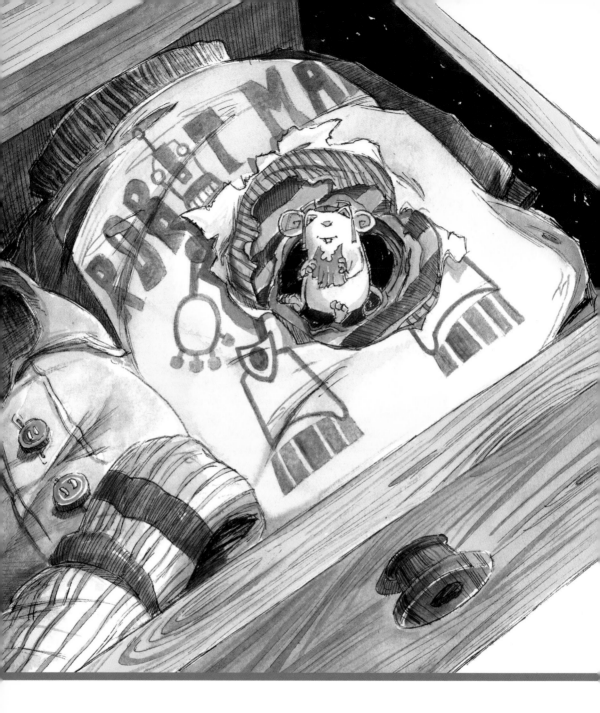

The mouse would race across my toes.
It liked to chew on all my clothes.
It liked to hide. It came and went, . . .

and with my shirt
it made a tent.

It frightened dad. He threw a mop.
The mouse got dad to blow his top.
It startled mom. She danced a jig.

The mouse made mother flip her wig.

Mom tossed a skate. Dad froze in place.
And that's when Kitty joined the chase.
As Kitty Cat searched on with me, . . .

8

… the mouse just hid
and had hot tea.

While Kitty made a great big fuss,
the mouse just sat and laughed at us.
It popped a hatch and left its cave.

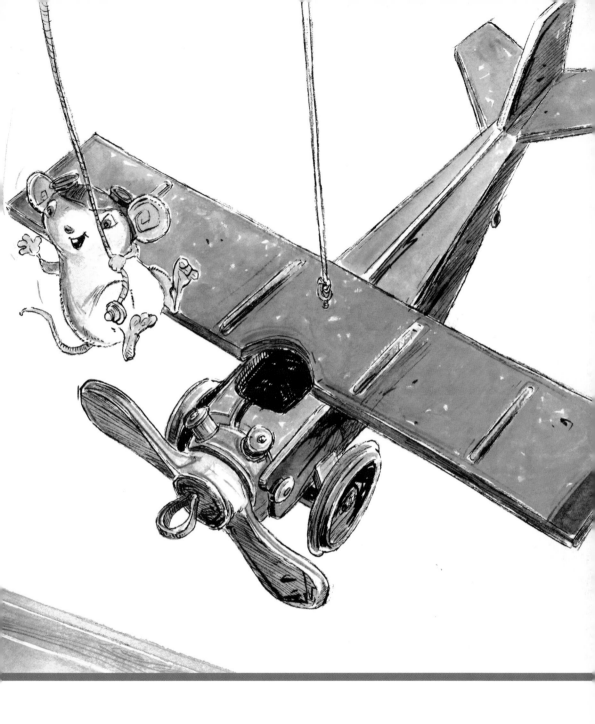

It swung up high
and gave a wave.

11

Mom saw the mouse and threw a can.
Dad dropped his cup and tossed a pan.
They filled the floor with pads of glue.

They stuck on dad—
and mother too.

The mouse ran swiftly up the sink.
It gave a smirk and then a wink.
The mouse sprayed Kitty with a hose.

This gave the cat
a big wet nose.

While Kitty tucked her tail in tears,
the mouse just grinned from ear to ear.
As Kitty cried, I hatched a plan.

I spun around
and off I ran.

I grabbed some cheese. I set a trap.
And when I heard the mouse trap snap,
I heard a howl. I heard a wail.

I got no mouse—
just Kitty's tail.

We chased the mouse beneath a chair.
But when Dad looked, it was not there.
I tried to trap it in a bowl.

 The mouse ran back
into its hole.

As Mom was resting unaware,
the mouse was nibbling on a pear.
It spit the seeds inside Mom's sock.

And then the mouse
ran up the clock.

We trapped it in a corner spot.
The mouse tied Kitty up in knots.
It bopped me on my big old head.

It rang the chime
and then it fled.

Down the stairway near the den,
the mouse was on the loose again.
I jumped the rail and leaped out far . . .

... and got the mouse
inside a jar.

We all hopped in my father's truck.
And now the mouse was one sad duck.
We drove as far as one could see, . . .

and then we let the
mouse go free.

The mouse made friends with other mice.
The country mice were really nice.
They ran all night and slept all day.

They liked to dance.
They liked to play.

At first the mouse was glad to roam,
but soon enough it missed our home.
So with some friends it hit the road, . . .

and on a tractor
they all rode.

They slipped inside a **farmer**'s shed.
They had a feast and went to bed.
The cows and chickens gave a shout.

The **farmer** came
and ran them out.

They hopped a train. They rode a bus.
They asked for help from Mailman Gus.
He checked his map. He scratched his ear, . . .

and then Gus led
them back to here.

There were a hundred, maybe more,
when all those mice ran through the door.
They dashed and darted up the wall, . . .

and then the mice
ran down the hall.

We chased them morning, noon, and night.
We would not quit without a fight!
They locked us out and we were beat, . . .

and so we moved
across the street.

If you liked **The Mouse in My House,** here is another We Both Read® Book you are sure to enjoy!

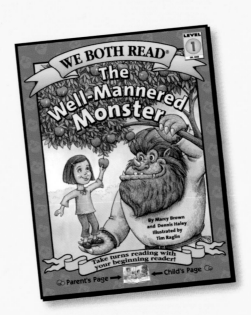

The Well-Mannered Monster

Matt may be a huge, hairy, green monster, but he is the nicest and best-mannered monster you will ever meet. Join Matt and his best friend, Pat, as they help Pat's mom get ready for a big dinner party. The dinner party guests don't know there will be a monster at the party, but Matt is so nice that hopefully everyone will like him and the party will go smoothly.